VANILLA & VINEGAR
~ A MEMOIR ~

JOSHUA J. DILBERT

Copyright © 2020 Joshua J. Dilbert.

All rights reserved. No part of this book may be reproduced, stored, or transmitted by any means—whether auditory, graphic, mechanical, or electronic—without written permission of the author, except in the case of brief excerpts used in critical articles and reviews. Unauthorized reproduction of any part of this work is illegal and is punishable by law.

This is a work of fiction. All of the characters, names, incidents, organizations, and dialogue in this novel are either the products of the author's imagination or are used fictitiously.

ISBN: 978-1-6847-1584-8 (sc)
ISBN: 978-1-6847-1585-5 (e)

Because of the dynamic nature of the Internet, any web addresses or links contained in this book may have changed since publication and may no longer be valid. The views expressed in this work are solely those of the author and do not necessarily reflect the views of the publisher, and the publisher hereby disclaims any responsibility for them.

Any people depicted in stock imagery provided by Getty Images are models, and such images are being used for illustrative purposes only. Certain stock imagery © Getty Images.

Lulu Publishing Services rev. date: 01/17/2020

Contents

Foreword vii
The Internship 1
The Fire Service 7
Aunt Cecilia 15
Numbers 21
Livin' On My Own 29
The Businessman 35
Back Home Again (#1) 41
My First Career 47
My Second Career 51
The Election Campaign 57
The Late Mr. Archer 63
Back Home Again (#2) 67
My Third Career 71

References 77

Foreword

I made my entrance into this world at the Faith Hospital in Cayman Brac, Cayman Islands, weighing 6 pounds, 5 ounces. The only child of Ralph and Charlene Bodden (née *Martin*), it did come with a few perks. I didn't have to be involved in any sibling wars and received every ounce of attention they could give.

I sometimes wonder what it's like to have a sibling, but I suppose it wasn't meant to be. At age eighteen, I finally deduced why I was an only child; it had to be my parents' ages at the time of my birth. After all, my mother was thirty-eight and my father was forty-two.

My parents met on Valentine's Day 1992, at the Coral Isle Club. Out of absent-mindedness, she left her purse unattended and my father returned it to her. Knowing instantly that she was the one, he asked her to dance and the rest is history. If I remember correctly the song they danced to was 'Hold On To The Nights' by Richard Marx. After a two-year courtship, they were married on 19 March 1994. I was born on 17 March 1995, just two days shy of their first wedding anniversary.

My father had been a cook aboard the Caldeman, now decommissioned, before retiring from his seafaring career and joining the Public Works Department. My mother had been a cashier at

Kirkconnell Ltd, a supermarket in Cayman Brac, but stopped working shortly after my birth. She had no intention of quitting her job, but my father convinced her so she could stay home and care for me. This was a remarkable feat given my mother's independent mindset. He told her that they could make do on his salary alone, especially since he was up for a promotion at work. However, he never got it.

That was in the good old days when we lived with my aunt Carlene. Battling stage four pancreatic cancer at the time, she was forced to retire under medical leave. With her mortgage payments being higher than her monthly pension, she was forced to swallow her pride and seek assistance from social services. My father insisted that he could help pay her monthly bills and the mortgage, but Aunt Carlene's pride would not permit that. Instead, my father only ended up giving her a 'pittance' of $150.00, the highest that she would allow him to give her.

When I was eleven months old, Aunt Carlene finally succumbed to her cancer diagnosis, aged fifty-seven. Within months the house foreclosed, and my father decided to buy her home back from the bank. Barely qualifying for the mortgage, the financial woes started almost at once. He was oblivious to the cost of paying a mortgage and keeping up a home. That meagre 'pittance' had insulated him from major expenses and gave him a rose-tinted view of his sister's precarious finances.

My father would later learn that Aunt Carlene was having difficulty keeping up the home after her husband of twenty-eight years left her for a local harlot. With two salaries, the costs of keeping up the house were manageable. With her husband out of the picture, her salary as a lowly office clerk couldn't pay the bills and her cancer diagnosis only compounded her burgeoning financial situation. Within a year, my father was forced to rethink and encourage his wife to seek employment.

However, luck was not on her side and she eventually had to resort to odd jobs around the island to help make ends meet. She would often clean yards, paint graves and chop out land plots. She even taught piano for several years, using Aunt Carlene's Yamaha piano to her advantage.

At age four, I began attending Creek Primary School, a stone's throw from the family home in Cayman Brac's Creek district. In my opinion, I was an above-average student who enjoyed science and art but disliked mathematics and physical education. I disliked the latter more because I wasn't 'athletically inclined' as my father put it. He often remarked that it was probably genetic because he wasn't good at sports either. However, I was an avid reader from a very young age, enjoying it so much that I even read during class time. Focusing completely on whatever book I was interested in at the time, I kept it hidden in the book box of my chrome-framed student desk. I got away with it for aeons.

But that afternoon came when my Year 4 teacher caught on to what I was doing. I was reading a Hardy Boys book when she did something I will never forget. I didn't notice as she slowly came towards my desk, and none of my classmates forewarned me. Slapping her long chalkboard ruler on top of my desk, she got my full attention. My young heart beat loudly in my ears as I stared into her stern, wrinkled face. She smelled faintly of cigarettes, which she smoked off-premises during lunch.

"From now on, you're banned from reading," she said quietly yet sternly.

"Yes Mam," I said, shaking like a duck in search of water.

She would retract the ban the next morning, on the condition that I never read again while she was teaching. Thankfully, at the end of Year 5, she retired, and the embargo officially ended. I would graduate primary school at the end of Year 6 and enter the-then Cayman Brac High School (now Layman E. Scott Sr. High School). The transition to high school was billed as gradual, but almost immediately I was barely passing my subjects.

However, it was not only academics however that drew concern. I was also one of the shortest pupils in the whole school. Luckily I wasn't actually picked on, but I was almost a social apparition. Eventually, things turned around. I managed to make a few older friends, became more comfortable in school and more focused on my schoolwork. Despite my shyness, I got involved in a number of extracurricular activities and passed all of my school-leaving examinations, graduating with eight high-level certificates. After six years of secondary school, graduation night had finally arrived. Standing in front of the microphone on stage, it was the most nervous I had ever been then.

Dressed in my scratchy blue graduation gown, I was now on the cusp of adulthood. Taking an audible deep breath into the microphone, it produced several seconds of ear-bleeding feedback, which fueled my anxiety more. When it subsided, I began reading the vote of thanks that I was tasked with writing. This was at the urging of school principal Mr. Cummings who thought I had underrated writing skills. Maybe it was all those essays I wrote during detention in his office. I was expecting to make a complete fool of myself but surprised myself when I read it flawlessly.

The audience clapped and cheered as I returned to my seat, an affirmation that I had done a good job. Minutes later the class of 2012 officially graduated, and we all turned our tassels proudly to the right to indicate such. It was almost over, but I still had to endure the crowd of people congratulating me, and of course those bloody photographs. Frankly, I thought that the graduation ceremony was unnecessary. Why couldn't it have been like yesteryear - before the influx of the North American hype? Why couldn't you just collect your diploma and call it a day? I kept telling myself that it would soon be over.

We, the graduating class, stood outside the Aston Rutty Centre and waited for the crowd to exit the building. The first person to approach me was my Chemistry teacher, Mr. Hilhorst, whom I could not stand. His stern, rough around the edges approach made him unpopular with most of the students actually. But in hindsight, he was precisely the teacher we needed. Almost everyone under his tutelage passed Chemistry with flying colours.

"Congrats son," he said, shaking my hand firmly. "What's the plan from here?"

"Well I'm gonna try for one of those government internships," I said. "By the time that finishes, something should come up in the fire service. They're supposed to be hiring new recruits next year."

"Come on!" Mr. Hilhorst blurted. "Why don't you go away to college? Try for one of those government scholarships. I know you have it in you."

No one supported my aspiration to become a firefighter it seemed and I couldn't understand why. After all, it was a lifetime job with excellent pay, excellent benefits and not to mention generous overtime. Perhaps everyone would warm up to the idea later.

"I'm so proud of you!" my mother said elatedly, hugging me after Mr. Hilhorst moved on to congratulate the others.

My father had on his signature formal event wear; an oversized light blue tuxedo he had bought from a yard sale about ten years ago. I was secretly embarrassed by the tuxedo, but at least no one made any snide remarks about it. Much like myself, he hated formalwear. The three of us went back into the building once the photographer had finished setting up his equipment, waiting around until we were called to take those bloody photographs.

The Internship

Days later, I sat on the front porch as usual. I was waiting for my father to arrive so we could have dinner. In accordance with my mother's rule, we only ate once all three of us were at the dinner table, one of us prayed before eating, and the television was turned off. Just before dusk, my father sped into the yard, parking the faithful family car underneath the guinep tree. In all the time it had been there, long before Aunt Carlene built the house, it hadn't borne one single guinep. My mother always mentioned that it couldn't bear any fruit because it was a 'he'. My father constantly threatened to get the useless tree chopped down, but my mother always talked him out of it because it provided shade for the car.

Now it wasn't that our burgundy 1987 Buick LeSabre was fresh off the assembly line. I was seven years old when my father purchased it. It was sun-bleached and covered with dents from then, but it ran well up until this point. The air conditioning had gone out so long ago that we eventually got used to not having it. My father always said that someday, when we ran into a little money, he would get it fixed. However, he still hadn't gotten around to it after all that time.

He took a while to come out of the vehicle, opening all the

envelopes he had gotten out of the post office box that day. I was a little annoyed because I wanted him to come in so I could eat

Despite their financial difficulties, my parents were lucky to get a windfall every now and then. But the overriding factor; they just weren't good with money! Or maybe they had different priorities. No matter how much money came their way; they would never put it to good use or save it or try to make it stretch. They would live rich for a few days until the money was squandered and they were back to square one.

Anyway, let's discuss this latest job opportunity.

There was my father, clutching a large manila envelope in his hand. Seeing me in the chair, my father plopped it right in my lap.

"Fill out these forms as soon as possible," he decreed. "The quicker I can get them back to the government administration building the better."

Carefully opening the envelope I saw it was a government employment application with the word 'INTERN' handwritten in the top left-hand corner. I wondered if he could secure a second form for the fire service.

"Do you think you get a second form for me?" I asked.

"What do you mean a second form?" he asked in a gruff tone of voice.

"For the fire service," I said. "They're gonna be looking new recruits soon."

"You're still fixated on that?"

"What do you mean?" I said. "I've always been serious about it!"

"You wanna be serious?" he said. "Apply for this internship, save some money, try to get into one of those big universities up in the States and get yourself a damn degree! It's not that hard to get a scholarship these days. Government is giving them away like damn Credit Union pens!"

"But I don't want to go to college!" I retorted. "I'm just not cut out for it! High school was hard enough for me. And besides, you didn't go to college and you turned out alright!"

"You really think I turned out alright?" he said with a huge sigh. "I work twice as hard as those damn college graduates and probably earn about a third of the pay. Working in that hot sun five days a week making eight dollars an hour is rough."

"What's wrong with that?" I asked.

"I don't want that for you, Danny," he said. "I don't want you to settle. Learn from our mistakes. I want better for you. Go to college, get your degree, make the big bucks. Think about it."

"But look at all the people that didn't go to college," I said, trying to reason with him. "They're still making a living."

"Those folks have been going to the same dead-end job for the past twenty-five years," he said. "And I bet they haven't gotten a single raise in ten years, even with the government. And forget about the private sector because you'll probably make the same salary your whole life. Worse yet, inflation will be lowering its value year after year."

I stayed quiet, a clear giveaway I would not be accepting his viewpoint. But he continued talking, oblivious to my reaction. Either that or he still hoped that his rationale would filter in.

"Son, when I got out of school government wasn't giving away money to send kids off to college," he said. "Young men went to sea or took the first job that came along. It doesn't have to be that way these days. There's more opportunity now; you need to grasp it."

I kept quiet.

"I know you're not interested in what I'm saying," he said rightly. "I don't expect you to understand right now. But you'll thank me later."

I wasn't interested in doing the damn internship, but to appease my father I decided to at least fill out the application and keep it on my nightstand until I could think up a reasonable excuse to get out of it. As I completed the damn form at my desk, I saw my father smoking a cigarette outside. Seeing me through the window, he put his index finger on his lips for a few seconds, indicating that I shouldn't mention anything about him smoking. This was because he had told my mother that he quit for good. This wasn't the case of course, but I wasn't concerned about that at this point. Within an hour the form was filled out and I fell asleep shortly after.

When I awoke the next morning, I grabbed my water on the nightstand and noticed that the form was gone from my desk. Realising what had happened, I trudged into the kitchen annoyed. There was my mother, just my mother, struggling to get a tin of corned beef open.

"Was someone in my room last night?" I asked.

"No...I don't think so anyway," like she was hiding something from me. "Why do you ask, you lost something?"

"I left something on my desk last night and now I can't find it. Where's Dad?"

"He had to go to work early," she said. "Want some breakfast?"

Realising what had happened, I returned to my room in a foul mood. My father never went to work early in the twenty-five years he had been employed with Public Works. But I suppose he had a good reason to get up early. Apparently, he had tiptoed into the room and taken the form off the desk whilst I slept.

That evening he returned home, parking underneath the barren guinep tree as usual. He had yet another massive manila envelope in hand as previously, placing it directly in my lap as before.

"You'll thank me later," he reminded me, patting the top of my head like when I was a little boy.

Much like graduation, there wasn't going to be an easy way out of this either. Still a minor and under my parents' roof, I would have to do this internship against my will. They were guaranteed internships as long as enough positions were available for all the applicants.

As a matter of fact, you didn't even have to do an interview. They simply informed you that they were willing to give you a placement, however, you didn't find out your placement until orientation day. Not really the best system but it enabled young graduates to earn some money until they could pursue other options such as going to university or permanent employment.

Orientation day arrived. A large crowd of us interns waited outside the government administration building in Stake Bay. Around half of the cohort included myself and a slew of my former classmates. Preference had been given to us, the most recent high school graduates, and those who had already filtered through the internship programme were slowly being passed up.

Finally, at twenty-two minutes past eight, the administration manager arrived and unlocked the glass doors that led inside. We all crowded into the cramped second-floor conference room and sat through an entire day of orientation. Eventually, we were each given a tiny piece of paper that had our placement written on it. My tiny piece of paper directed me to the post office at West End, which wasn't what I wanted to do at all.

Though I grumbled about it at first, I really began getting into the swing of things after the first few weeks. I remember waiting patiently for lunch, not having much to eat for breakfast that morning as we ran out of propane for our stove. My usual meal of cornmeal porridge was downgraded to toast. When the clock struck noon, my supervisor exited her tiny office with her handbag slung around her shoulder, a sign that she was going to lunch.

"You need a ride anywhere for lunch?" she asked.

"Not today, I'm just gonna grab something from the store," I told her, which was just across from the post office.

After buying two beef patties and a can of Pepsi from the Market Place supermarket, I took a seat on the wooden bench outside the store. I ate quietly and headed back to work, hoping that my supervisor had returned so she could let me in the cool building. I hated getting hot and sweaty in a long sleeve shirt, and the sun was brutally hot for October. As I walked back, I heard someone shout my name from the nearby bush. It turned out to be my best friend Anthony. There he was, underneath a tree, drinking a Heineken. Even though we weren't of legal age yet, Anthony had no problem securing alcohol.

"You want one?" he asked, taking one of the greenies of his backpack.

"Where the hell did you get those from?" I asked, interested in how he got this alcoholic beverage despite being underage.

"Don't you worry about that," he assured me. "Do you want one or not?"

"Alright, I'll have one," I said, accepting it for the sake of looking cool.

I drank mine quickly, hoping to finish it by the time my supervisor's vehicle turned into the car park. At work and in the comfort of air-conditioning, I felt a bit sleepy, trying to a quick snooze in the corner before the last dispatch.

The Fire Service

It was the final day of my government internship. Though I enjoyed the post office somewhat, I could now set my eyes on the fire service. Loud fire engines, gallons and gallons of spraying water, and dominoes most important. To celebrate the end of another step in my life, I wanted a night on the town.

All the 'ex-interns' would be spending the last of their internship money at the Coral Isle Club. I heard that the fire service would be seeking trainees within the next couple of months. With my application form nearly completed, I was only waiting for the day that the advert came out in the paper. My father bought a newspaper every day, and I looked through them religiously, hoping to come across the advert and then submit my application.

My parents didn't turn in until close to eleven that night, which was cutting it close because Anthony was due to pick me up at eleven-thirty. In the meantime, just for the hell of it, I stole one of my father's cigarettes out of the kitchen cupboard. I then exited the house quietly through my bedroom window, careful not to brush against the prickly bougainvillea that grew against the house.

I had never smoked a cigarette before, but there's a first time for everything. Stealing one out of my father's pack, I put it into my pants pocket. I always wondered what it was like to smoke a cigarette. It looked cool when others did it, and doing so might just bring me into the fold. I was aware of the health risks but chose to turn a blind eye. You weren't somebody it seemed unless you had a bad habit of some sort.

By the time we reached Coral Isle most of the crowd was hanging around in the car park. They had become bored of the DJ playing reggae and found more enjoyment shooting the breeze outside. Pulling the now bent cigarette out of my pocket, all went silent.
"*Am I really doing this?*" I thought to myself, looking at this tiny white cylinder between my index and middle finger.
"Danny, what the hell are you doing with that?" Anthony asked incredulously.
"Well there's a first time for everything," I announced. "Gimme a light!"
Anthony did not hesitate. He wasted no time in lighting up that bent cigarette for me. I coughed violently as I sucked on the cigarette and the smoke entered my lungs. Still, there was no turning back from the beginning of "cool".
Time flies when you're having fun. The bar has now closed and everyone was trying to get home. Taking a seat on one of the parking blocks, I waited on Anthony as he tried to get the barmaids' numbers without success.
I felt a hard jab in my lower back.
"Shit!" I said, quickly rubbing the precise spot where he poked me. "You scared me half to death!"
"That was kind of the idea!" Anthony replied cackling. "You ready to go?"
I got back into the station wagon and we sped along the north side of the island. Every home was in complete darkness. Everyone was fast asleep.

"How the hell did you end up with that cigarette?" asked Anthony, as I watched the speedometer go past eighty kilometers an hour.

The increasing speed frightened the shit out of me, but I couldn't let him know.
"I stole one of Dad's cigarettes from out of the cupboard," I said.
"I should have known," he said. "But I hope you know that smoking is bad for your health. You're gonna die of cancer."
"Stop talking shit!" I blurted. "You smoke too!"
Anthony let out a devilish laugh, having foreseen my reply. When we reached the road that ran past my house, I saw to it that Anthony turned his lights off. I tiptoed through the yard and entered my bedroom through the window, again trying to avoid the prickly bougainvillea that my mother had planted right against the window. I wondered if she had planted it there intentionally, anticipating nights like these. I was practically tapped awake later that morning by my mother.
"What the hell is that for?" I said sharply, still in bed.
"Honey, we're just going out for errands," Mother said, almost whispering. "Would you like to come along?"
"No!" I moaned, covering myself with the bedspread.
"We're gonna be a little while," she advised. "Your breakfast is in the microwave when you get hungry."
I remained silent, my head hurting from a hangover. When I was sure my parents were gone, I slowly made my way to the kitchen to pinch another one of my father's cigarettes. Anthony had told me that the nicotine would help relieve hangovers, which I would soon discredit. Unfortunately, the pack was empty and he had the audacity to just leave the hollow pack there. That meant I would have to walk down to the liquor store to purchase another one, hungover and in the broiling heat.

Luckily, it was only five minutes away.
I walked inside the old wooden structure, catching sight of the

owner reading yesterday's newspaper at the counter. Customers often asked her why she didn't build a newer, more modern store. Apparently, that had been the dream of her parents, planning to build a larger store on another piece of land adjacent. She had the same pat answer, telling them that the building was her last remaining connection to her deceased parents. When she was growing up, they operated it as a modest dry-goods store and when they passed on, she turned it into a liquor store.

"You got any small B&H?" I asked.

"Yes we do," she said, taking a pack from under the counter.

I gave her a crumpled five-dollar note, my hands shaking like a leaf, and she handed me the pack.

"Hungover?" she questioned.

"You bet ma'am," I said.

"Bobo, drink more!" she said laughing. "That's how I get over my hangovers."

Regrettably, Mrs. Heston walked in as I placed the pack into my pocket. She was the last person on earth I wanted to run into, especially at the liquor store. She loved nothing more than to make my blood boil.

"Don't tell me you're doing that too!" she spouted.

"No ma'am...this is for someone else," I said, thinking on my feet. "He says he's going to pay me back."

"Well I hope so," interjected the owner. "You know how that goes these days."

"Well whoever you're getting it for, they need to come and buy it their own damn self," Mrs. Heston said. "And for God's sake, try and stay outta this place. Drinking and smoking are not good, ya hear."

I left the store in disgust, turning around in time to see the owner giving Mrs. Heston her usual large pack of Rothmans. She thought that I didn't see, but I watched as she quickly placed it into her handbag. She didn't want anyone to know that she was a smoker, even though it was common knowledge.

I headed home, walking through a large tract of land that had recently been cleared for a new public park. There was a groundbreaking ceremony almost a year before, but nothing had happened since. Much of the bush had already regrown. I could see two people in the distance, standing around a station wagon. I knew the car however I couldn't tell exactly who the people were. When I got close enough, I realised it was Anthony and Adrian. I disliked Adrian but tried to tolerate him because of my long-standing friendship with Anthony. Standing at a distance close enough for them to see, I took a cigarette out of the pack and lit it just to show off.

"Hey, come here!" shouted Anthony.

I sauntered towards them

"How are you liking the blends?" Adrian asked.

"Not so bad you know."

"I remember my first time," he said chuckling. "It was about six months ago. My brother got me into it. The first couple of times I coughed myself nearly to death!"

Adrian nudged Anthony slightly, indicating that there was something important that they needed to tell me.

"Hey listen, we're going on a little mission later," he said. "We're going to egg Mrs. Heston's house at midnight. You game?"

It was fifteen minutes past midnight before the headlights of Anthony's station wagon came into view. I hoped that my parents didn't decide to check up on me. A quick fifteen-minute drive brought us to Mrs. Heston's house, mostly unchanged since it was built in the late 1950s. Her humble abode was almost in complete darkness, except for a lone outdoor light that shone above the front door. Her teal 1984 Lincoln town car was in the carport, an indicator that she was home sleeping.

Mrs. Heston was a sarcastic, uncouth woman. She had been widowed ever since her husband Mr. Heston passed away from mesothelioma eight years earlier, blamed on the asbestos he was exposed to as a seaman. Though she received over one million dollars in a settlement, she hadn't spent any of her settlement money it seemed. Her home was falling apart, her vehicle was always in the garage, and her wardrobe needed some serious updating. She always dressed like it was the sixties, replete with stirrup pants and high neck blouses.

She was as parsimonious and antisocial as you can imagine. Rumour had it she lived off of condensed soup and table water crackers. Apparently, she had a son living in California who worked as an actuary but I never recalled seeing him.

Anthony opened the trunk to reveal several dozen cartons of eggs. Starting with one box each, we proceeded to throw the eggs against the house. But our excitement came to an abrupt end when a light came on. We all froze, hoping she wouldn't come outside. But unfortunately, she did…shotgun in hand.

"Get off my goddamn property before I blow you to bits!" she shouted.

"Bitch!" shouted Adrian, before the three of us bolted for the station wagon.

Unluckily, she spotted me.

"Daniel Bodden, you little bastard!" she bellowed. "I'm calling your parents!"

As we sped away, nearly running over a stop sign in the process, I hoped that she was bluffing.

"She doesn't have their number," I thought. *"And how would she know?"*

I had barely entered through the bedroom window when I heard it.

"Danny, get your ass in this living room right now!" my father shouted.

Walking out of my bedroom and into the living room, I found my parents sitting silently and stiffly on the living room sofa, waiting patiently for my return.

"Where the hell have you been, boy?" my father questioned. "Because I know you ain't been sleeping in that room!"

I stayed quiet.

"The last time I checked your vocal cords were in tip-top condition!" my mother blurted. "Now spit it!"

"Oh, Christ, the phonebook!" I remembered internally. *"I forgot about that."*

"We were out egging Mrs. Heston's house," I said slowly.

"I can't believe this!" my mother shouted, getting up from the couch. "My son is sneaking out egging peoples houses, drinking all hours of the night, and smoking, you think we didn't know?"

"Honey, let's discuss the egging situation before we get into anything else," my father said. "Mrs. Heston just called us and she is pissed! She almost pressed charges but lucky for you I got her to change her mind."

"Oh thank God!" I said with a sigh of relief.

"Your ass is not off the hook yet!" my father warned. "You and your friends are gonna clean up your damn mess! You have to clean the egg stains off her house and then you have to clean her yard! You're gonna rake the leaves; trim the hedges, the whole nine yards. That yard should be spick and span by the time you get through. Do you understand?"

"All of that?" I asked.

"Do you understand?" my father said a little more firmly.

"Yes I understand!" raising my voice. I was not pleased as you can imagine, but I was still fortunate that the police didn't get involved.

"Bobo, you're a lucky boy tonight," my mother said.

"What's gotten into you?" my father questioned. "I can't get over this one. But no more. We've had enough of this. The sneaking out, the drinking, the smoking…it's going to end before it becomes a habit. We mightn't be able to control you anymore, but we're gonna give the job to someone who can!"

"Who?" I asked.

"Your Aunt Cecilia," he said.

Aunt Cecilia

Aunt Cecilia was an ambitious, no-nonsense woman. At the age of eighteen, she moved from Cayman Brac over to Grand Cayman, settling in the district of West Bay. Moving from job to job, always in search of higher pay, she managed to save enough money to owner finance a parcel of land. Slowly she built a small store from the ground up, and then her home behind it. Eventually, she quit all her half-assed jobs and became an entrepreneur.

I didn't always get along with Aunt Cecilia. Whenever we went to visit her or vice versa, one week was enough for me. We often clashed over the simplest of things. Don't get me wrong, I loved Aunt Cecilia but I just couldn't imagine living with her for any longer than a week. She was always congenial at the beginning of the trip, but within a week's time, she would become miserable and controlling. Hopefully, my father was being impulsive and wouldn't follow through with the threat.

Before I knew it, I was at the airport.

"This is for the best, son," my mother said, hugging me tightly at the airport. "I know that you're a good child. You can be anything you wanna be."

My father didn't have much to say for once. He just hugged me and sent me on my way. I looked at the island landscape as the Saab aircraft lifted into the air. Twenty-five minutes later, the plane landed at Owen Roberts International Airport in George Town, Grand Cayman. I picked up my suitcases from the baggage carousel and walked straight outside. Sure enough, there was Aunt Cecilia right outside.

"Who is this handsome young man coming towards me? she joked. "But you're still a tad too thin. I must fatten you up a bit."

Arriving at her house in West Bay fifteen minutes later, I found it immaculate as always. Aunt Cecilia was a self-proclaimed neat freak; at times I suspected she was bordering on obsessive-compulsive disorder. The bed was perfectly spread. The dresser was completely devoid of clutter. There wasn't a speck of dust to be found. There was no way that a home could be so tidy.

"I gotta check on something at the store," she said suddenly, as I marvelled at the cleanliness. "You can get settled in the guest bedroom okay?"

Later that evening I sat with Aunt Cecilia at the dining room table, knowing that she would probably probe into my life back home.

"What's going on with you?" she asked. "Your parents had quite a story to tell when they called me the other day."

"What exactly did they tell you?" I asked sheepishly.

"Lots of things," she said. "But I wanna hear it from your mouth."

I took a deep sigh and began to speak.

"Well, for starters, I snuck out of the house to egg Mrs Heston's house," I said.

"You mean that old lady with the old house on Republic Lane?"

"Exactly!" I said. "Wait a minute, you know her?"

"Know her?" she said. "She taught me piano when I was in primary school! I always hated her and learning the piano. She was always shouting at me! Your grandmother forced me to do it. I can't believe Mrs Heston is still alive! She was old even way back when!"

"Who knows she's probably a vampire," I joked.

"True!" she replied, laughing.

"Well, my friends and I planned it," I explained. "We snuck out and egged her house. We almost got away with it, but then she came out and recognized who I was. She called my parents, they freaked out, and here I am."

"You didn't wear a mask?" she asked.

"No, why?"

"Oh my dear sweet nephew!" she said chuckling. "Don't you know to at least cover your face when egging someone's house?"

"You don't sound upset," I asked

"Of course not!" she said, chuckling. "That is just a part of growing up. I did all sorts of crazy shit when I was your age. There were many nights when I drank until I threw up. I used to smoke weed too."

"You're joking!" I blurted, not believing what I was hearing.

"I'm not joking," she said. "But the weed wasn't a regular thing you know, every once in a while. Your father was even worse than I was! He tried anything and I mean anything. I think he even snorted cocaine once or twice. But for God's sake don't tell him I told you!"

I nodded slowly, indicating I would not.

"Listen, I've given this some thought," she said, putting her hand on top of mine. "I don't think you're as bad as your parents make you out to be. This is just 'young man shenanigans' as I call it. Plus you know that your parents are melodramatic anyhow. But I think a little time away from home will do you some good. Time to grow up, find out who you are, sort yourself out."

I didn't say anything, trying to think about it.

"Is that okay," she said softly.

"I'm okay with it," I said. "But what am I going to do here?"

"Don't worry, I have that covered!" she assured me.

That Monday morning, at 8AM sharp, Aunt Cecilia had me start work at her store Cecilia's, aptly named after the woman herself. For the first two hours, not a single customer came in. I was beginning to wonder if the store got any business at all. Finally, a customer entered, chatting away on her cellphone.

"I'm gonna check him tonight!" she said as she dumped several individual packs of potato chips on the counter.

"You know what? I'm gonna put a couple of dollars on 12 and 21," she said. "It's Lipton Bar on Campbell Drive, that's where he sells from. It's the burgundy building with all the little wooden cabanas in front. He owns the place."

She placed a crumpled ten dollar note on the counter, which I tried to smooth out before placing it into the cash register. I gave the lady her change as she moved the phone away from her ear. Finally, she had the common decency to address me.

"Thanks, you hear," she whispered.

It was that phone conversation piqued my interest in the 'numbers'. I decided to investigate and walked to Lipton Bar after work.

'Numbers' was, and still is, the underground lottery of the Cayman Islands. Though highly illegal under the Gambling Law, that didn't stop it from becoming a growing business, operating in contravention of an archaic law I dare say.

It was punishable by law and anyone caught keeping a gaming house could face a fine of four hundred Cayman Islands dollars or twelve months imprisonment with or without hard labour. While the Gambling Law did allow for non-profit organizations to conduct raffles, and ships with onboard casinos to be exempt from the gambling ban, any person caught playing in a gaming house could face a fine of ten Cayman Islands dollars or two months imprisonment with or without hard labour.

Forget about it being enforced though - no one I knew had ever paid a fine or gone to jail for it.

I finally made my way Lipton Bar. It had been in business for over thirty years and was also the headquarters of Mr. Lipton's illegal numbers operation. I entered the dark premises, finding the place empty. A scantily clad barmaid was behind the counter, wiping wine glasses with a white tea towel.

"Where do I buy the numbers?" I asked her discreetly.

"Go through that door right there," she said pointing behind her. "You can just go inside, he won't mind."

Heading towards the wooden door I saw 'J.A. LIPTON' written on it in black marker pen. Turning the knob slowly, I entered to find the very same lady who was on the phone at the store that morning. She was seated on the other side of Mr. Lipton's desk, writing down the numbers she wanted to buy on a torn piece of white printer paper. Sitting next to her was a young lady who I guessed was probably around my age with frizzy brown hair.

I remember exactly what she was wearing. It wasn't anything special, just a plain white t-shirt and a pair of light blue jeans. But there was just something about her that captivated me. The two ladies quickly did their business and left.

"Hello young man," Mr. Lipton addressed me. "What can I do for you?"

"I wanna put five dollars on 12 and 21," I said confidently

"Three in a row!" he said. "The two ladies just bought those exact numbers. Makes me believe it's coming tonight you know!"

Just then his cell phone vibrated loudly in the top drawer of his desk.

"Excuse me, I have to take this," he said.

I really didn't pay any attention to the first bit of Mr. Lipton's conversation, choosing instead to stare at the various fine art prints he had hanging throughout the office. But then something piqued my interest.

"Yeah buddy, I'm still looking for an agent," he said. "You know how it is. Just gotta find someone I can trust...I'll keep you posted."

As soon as I heard that, the thought of becoming an agent for Mr. Lipton took hold. It seemed like an excellent opportunity - too good to pass up. In retrospect, if I had even an inkling of what would have happened down the road, I would never have done it. But I'm jumping ahead of myself.

"I couldn't help but overhear you on the phone, Mr. Lipton," I said, putting myself forward. "Perhaps I could be your agent?"

"You really wanna be my agent?" he asked like it was an unrealistic prospect.

"Yes," I said.

"Well, to be honest, I've never had anyone as young as you," he said. "How old are you anyhow…if you don't mind me asking?"

"I just turned eighteen," I said.

"Wow, that's very young still," he said. "But I will think about it. Check me here tomorrow evening around this time. I should have a decision by then."

As it turned out, twelve was the winning number that night, exactly as Mr. Lipton had predicted. The next evening I entered his office anxious, hoping to collect my winnings and find out if I got the job.

"Here you go young man," said Mr. Lipton, taking some money out of his desk drawer and placing it in front of me. "That's five hundred dollars right there. Count it for yourself. But you should make a lot more when you become my agent."

"Seriously?" I asked, after counting five one-hundred-dollar bills.

"You can even start tonight," he said.

Numbers

Before I knew it, Mr. Lipton dropped me off at the West Bay Beach, about a ten-minute drive away from the bar.

"I'll pick you up around ten!" he shouted over the sound of the truck engine.

Taking a seat underneath one of the cabanas, I waited for these so-called customers to show up. All I had was a brand new composition book and a deposit bag with eighty dollars in petty cash. It was fairly simple recordkeeping; I just wrote down their names, the numbers they purchased, how much money they put towards each of the numbers, and their phone number so I could get in touch with them in case they won.

Not even ten minutes after I arrived, customers started coming out of nowhere. I was literally trembling the whole night. You never knew if a customer would inform the police or if a customer was actually the police. It was tricky and I didn't quite know who to trust. By the time Mr. Lipton returned to pick me up, the pouch was crammed with cash and the composition book was already half-way written through. We made it back to the bar discreetly.

"Lock the doors son!" he instructed. "No telling what might happen!"

We counted up the night's cash, some three thousand dollars. But we would still have to wait until someone called Mr. Lipton with the winning number. I never figured out who that person was, but that call never came in until minutes to twelve. He could have easily looked it up online, but Mr. Lipton wasn't into computers.

The numbers that Mr. Lipton played shadowed the Belizean lottery; the Boledo in fact. Luckily, only one person had bought the winning number. That was excellent because we had to pay out winnings at the rate of fifty dollars per dollar spent. In other words, they received 'x' amount of dollars spent times 50 (a little algebra there). Placing that person's winnings in a plain white envelope, we locked everything in his safe. As Mr. Lipton's sub-agent, I was entitled to thirty percent of the night's earnings. I received nine hundred dollars.

Feeling rather pleased with myself, I quietly entered Aunt Cecilia's house. I found her fast asleep on the sofa, the television still blasting. Turning it off, I quietly picked up her empty wine glass and placed it in the kitchen sink. I tiptoed to my bedroom, hoping that she wouldn't wake up and realised how late it was.

I went to work the next morning as usual. Aunt Cecilia didn't ask anything about how late I was, and I naturally kept mum about it. I was stocking shelves at the back of the store when I heard someone enter. I walked towards the checkout counter at the front, realizing immediately that it was the same girl I had seen in Mr. Lipton's office the other night...with a police vest on.

"Hey, do you sell lighters here?" she asked. "Like for cigarettes?"
"Yes we do," I said, placing one on the counter. "There you go."
"You look familiar," she said.
"So do you," I replied nervously.
"Wait a minute...didn't I see you at Lipton Bar the other night?"
"What are you doing with that vest on?" I asked.

"I'm a police trainee," she said, pointing at the vest with her acrylic nails.

"You're training to become a police officer and you buy numbers?"

"Yes," she said sheepishly. "But I'm trying to get it out of my system before I become a real officer. And you don't have to worry about me telling anybody, I promise I won't tell the guys back at work."

"Good to know," I said, handing the young lady her change. "I never got your name though."

"Amanda," she said looking at her wristwatch. "Listen, I really need to go okay. Thanks for your help."

Little did I know that I would run into Amanda again that night. When I finished the usual count-up with Mr. Lipton, I had over one thousand dollars on me. Finding Amanda sitting at the bar all alone, I took a seat next to her. Taking a crisp one-hundred-dollar note out of my wallet, I slapped it on the counter.

"Get this woman whatever she wants," I said when the bartender came towards me. "It's on me."

The bartender immediately went to get Amanda another drink.

"How's it going?" I asked.

"Not too much action here tonight," mumbled Amanda.

I realised that she had consumed quite a bit of alcohol by that point, but the bartender still placed the drink in front of her.

"How many of those have you had?" I asked.

"I don't remember..."

"After this drink, I'm taking you home," I asserted. "You've got work in the morning. You need to keep a clear head."

I took the liberty of walking her home, having my arm around her for nearly the whole walk. She didn't have any objection to it, so I just let it be.

"You can come inside you know," she said. "My parents won't be home until much, much later."

We sat on the bed in her bedroom, where she quickly took off her blouse and threw it on the floor. And now she was attempting to unclip her brassiere.

"What the hell are you doing?" I said.

"Danny, please make love to me," she begged.

I was surprised but eager. Then someone entered the house, spoiling the fun.

"Amanda where are you?" a female voice shouted.

Guessing it might be her mother; this was definitely the time to dip. Not wanting to take any chances, I vacated the premises via the bedroom window and headed home, almost twisting my ankle when I jumped out. When I returned home, Aunt Cecilia was in the kitchen drinking some tea.

"I've barely seen you recently," she said.

I didn't say anything.

"Look, I don't have a problem with you going out," she said. "You can do your thing as long as you're not doing anything illegal or dangerous or lewd."

"If you only knew," I thought to myself.

"But you should try to spend a little time with your aunt every now and then."

"We'll do something, real soon," I promised.

Several nights would follow with good commissions. Eventually, the night came when a lot of folks bought the winning number, and my commission ended up being a mere thirty bucks. Some weeks after, Amanda sauntered dejectedly towards the counter. Something was troubling her.

"Danny, is there something you want to tell me?" she asked.

"What are you talking about?"

"You don't know anything about numbers?" she asked.

I just looked at her puzzled, before it dawned on me.

"Oh shit!" I blurted.

"They suspect at work that Mr. Lipton is selling numbers," she said after a very brief but awkward silence. "You need to give him a head's up."

"I'll call him," I said grabbing for the shop phone.

"I would tell him in person if I were you," she cautioned before walking away.

"But Amanda, wait!" I pleaded, trying to get a better sense of the situation.

She didn't wait.

I decided to lock up the store to look for Mr Lipton, figuring that Aunt Cecilia would take quite a while running her errands. I hoped that she didn't return before I did, or I would never hear the end of it. Running into his office at breakneck speed, he looked quizzically over his reading glasses.

"Mr. Lipton, it's very important!" I blurted, out of breath from running.

"They're gonna raid me again, aren't they?" he said, taking a bottle of whiskey out of his desk and pouring it into a glass.

"Yes, they are," I said. "And I heard it from a pretty good source."

"Thank you for telling me," he said calmly. "You know what...take the night off tonight. You'll still get your thirty percent as always."

"Thank you, sir," I said, not understanding why he was taking it so lightly.

"You know son, I've been in this business twenty-seven years now," he said. "There ain't nothing I haven't seen. But whoever this guy is, they don't quite know how things work yet..."

"What does that mean?" I asked, still not understanding.

"I'll tell you some other time," he said, giving me a wink.

I reported for duty the next night. I couldn't understand why he wasn't worried.

"How did it go?" I said quietly.

"They came here with some bullshit warrant," he said. "Three of them searched in this office. One found a crumpled up receipt in the wastebasket. They took me to the police station, interrogated me for about an hour, and then they let me go. These were all new recruits... they don't know quite how things go yet."

"What are you talking about?" I asked.

"I have diplomatic immunity," he said. "The new ones don't know about it until they learn the ropes. It keeps me out of trouble."

"How the hell did you get diplomatic immunity?" I said, bluntly.

"Let's just say I have connections," he said. "It costs me an arm and a leg but it keeps the right fucking people quiet."

"How did you even get into numbers?"

"My brother got me into it," he said. "He lived in Belize for years; married a Belizean woman and had a son. When he came back to Cayman, he started selling the numbers, based off the Boledo. We were business partners and when he died, I still kept it going. But I guess you don't want to hear about that, so I'll just let you get on your rounds."

I could sense from Mr. Lipton's tone that this was a sensitive subject, but consciously noted to probe into it further. After our usual end-of-night count up, I received my commission and headed home. However, nothing could have prepared me for what would happen when I arrived home. Dressed in a silk nightgown, Aunt Cecilia rushed out of her bedroom fuming.

"Why you bastard!" she shouted, pushing her palms against my chest as if she wanted to push me down. "You really selling numbers now?"

"How did you know that?" I asked, not attempting to deny it.

"You think I wasn't going to find out?" she said. "There ain't nothing that goes on 'round this square that I don't hear about sooner or later! Especially when it concerns my family! How long have you been doing this anyhow?"

"Two months," I said quietly.

"You have been doing this for two months?" she asked rhetorically. I didn't say a word.

"Well I shall fix you!" she spewed. "Tomorrow morning I want your ass out! Pack your bags and go!"

"Aunt Cecilia, please!" I begged. "Don't be this way!"

"I want you out of here by twelve o'clock tomorrow afternoon!" she insisted.

Livin' On My Own

I will never forget the look on Aunt Cecilia's face. She just stood there motionless as I packed my belongings into the two suitcases I had. I walked out of the bedroom, trying hard not to look at her.

"You're a waste!" she said slowly but bitterly. "A fucking waste!"

Those words hurt me to the fucking core. It was like before Jesus's crucifixion when Pontius Pilate washed his hands and said 'it is your responsibility'. She was no longer responsible for me. I was the world's responsibility now, and whatever it had in store for me, good or bad, it didn't matter to Aunt Cecilia anymore.

I didn't have the faintest idea where I was gonna go. I didn't want to return to my parents and admit defeat, so I made my way to Lipton bar and hoped for the best. During that walk in the sweltering heat, two heavy suitcases in tow, no one offered a lift. I would have to swallow my pride and beg Mr. Lipton to take me in.

"Mr. Lipton, I have a problem," I announced, with two heavy suitcases.

"Not another bloody raid is it?"

"No," I clarified. "I need a place to stay."

"A place to stay? What the hell happened?"

I sat down timidly in front of Mr Lipton's desk.

"My aunt kicked me out today," I said.

"For what?"

"She found out that I'm selling numbers," she said. "And she went off on me."

He just stared at me.

"Look, if it's going to be a problem, I understand," I said.

"Not a problem," he said.

"Thank you so much, sir!" I said excitedly, like a kid in a candy store. "I really appreciate it! And I promise I won't be a bother. You won't even know I'm there."

"But only for a while," he uttered. "Just until you get on your feet. Tough love is the best, I have to make a man out of you."

That evening I climbed up the creaky wooden stairs of Mr Lipton's weather-beaten home in Birch Tree Hill, West Bay. I flopped onto the bed in one of his spare bedrooms and stared at the spinning ceiling fan. I was surprised that the man had a humongous four-bedroom, two-storey home. No wonder he was so willing to take me in; he had room to spare.

I must have fallen asleep as the clatter of breaking glass sprang me to consciousness. I ran down the stairs to find Mr. Lipton holding pieces of a broken coffee cup as he stared at a portrait in the living room.

"Are you alright, Mr. Lipton?" I asked him.

"I just dropped this cup that's all."

"What are you looking at?" I asked.

"Oh this is my ex-wife and my son," he said a slight smirk. "He must have been about six or seven then."

"Where are they now?"

"Your guess is as good as mine, son," he said with a sigh. "They don't want anything to do with me anymore."

"But they're your family aren't they?"

"The last time I checked," he said. "But, thinking back, I was an asshole. I drank a lot. I would lose my temper at the turn of a dime. I cheated on my wife over and over again. Just before she left, it seemed as if the cheating didn't even bother her anymore. Eventually, she stopped beating up the women and me of course."

"But you didn't hit her back though?" I asked, hoping the answer was no.

"I slapped her once, on the face," he admitted. "I hit her so hard I thought I had killed her. She was curled up on the ground writhing in pain."

"My God, what did you do then?"

"I just stood there and called her a stupid bitch," he said. "Then I just left her there sobbing on the floor."

"Then what happened?"

"Well that was the turning point for her," he admitted. "I went to open up the bar the next morning and she was in the kitchen trying to open a can of corned beef. Then when I returned that night, she and my son was gone."

"Have you seen them since?"

"I've only seen them twice; my son's high school graduation and his graduation from college. I don't even think they wanted me to come to that."

"I'm sorry to hear that," I said.

"Well I suppose I deserved it," he said. "Karma they call it. I'm going to bed now. Have a good night."

I now understood why Mr. Lipton was so bitter.

Weeks later, Amanda had finally completed her police training and today was her graduation from the Training & Development Unit of the Royal Cayman Islands Police Service. I sat quietly in the back row during the ceremony and even stuck around as she posed for photographs afterwards with her parents, brother, and grandmother. Romance was starting to blossom between us, but she didn't want her strict parents to know just yet. Although they were initially unhappy with her decision to become a police officer, they had no choice but to accept it. After the photographer showed them the pictures he had taken, the family walked out of the hall, Amanda winking at me as they crossed. She came back inside seconds later.

"You haven't told them yet, have you?" I asked.

"No," she said as she tiptoed and kissed my face. "I'll tell them soon though."

"What the hell are you waiting for?" I said. "You're twenty years old for God's sake! You're about to become a police officer. You could move out tomorrow and get a place of your own."

"You don't think that I know that already!" she said. "But I can't just up and go. I need to save some money before I can move out."

"Well, I don't know about you but I'm getting a place of my own," I said. "If you want to join me, be my guest."

"Wait a minute, you're moving out of your aunt's place?"

"My aunt kicked me out," I clarified. "I'm living with the boss until I can find a place of my own. Come with me nuh! I'll take care of everything!"

Just then we heard Amanda's mother's high heels clicking against the steep wheelchair ramp that led up to the main door of the building.

"I'll text you later!" she said, running out of the hall.

Amanda and I soon settled into a one-bedroom apartment in Windsor Park, much to the chagrin of Amanda's parents. Hence, I was surprised when Amanda came home some weeks later with some interesting news.

"My parents wanna meet you," she said, putting her arms around my neck while I was seated on the sofa.

"They really wanna meet me?" I asked, surprised that they finally succumbed, and secretly wondering what the change in attitude was.

"Yes," she said. "They're coming over for dinner tomorrow night. I have the day off tomorrow so I'm gonna cook and get this place cleaned up."

"But I'm busy tomorrow," I said.

"Call Mr. Lipton and tell him you need the night off," she said. "One night won't kill you, and it definitely won't kill him."

At Amanda's urging, I took the night off. Enduring a strained supper, I managed to convince her parents that I was a decent young man. As far as they knew, I worked as a filing clerk by day and took classes at the University College of the Cayman Islands by night. The façade was set.

As the weeks wore on, I decided to become my own numbers agent as opposed to just being a sub-agent for Mr. Lipton. It was a monumental risk without Mr. Lipton's financial backing and so-called 'diplomatic immunity' but I thought I was ready. Also, if I went off on my own I could have one hundred percent of the profits instead of just thirty percent.

The Businessman

"I don't know how to tell you this," I told Mr. Lipton one evening with a trembling voice. "I'm going off on my own."

"Son, I didn't think you had it in you!" he said, the complete opposite from what I was expecting. "But take a fool's advice. Be careful who you put your trust in. I don't need to tell you that."

With Mr. Lipton's blessing, I was determined to start the next chapter. For the first several weeks, profits were fairly good. Then the tables turned. Everyone started buying the winning number and for several days my profits began dwindling. Then, at the drop of a hat, profits increased again.

Some time later, I saw a missed call from my mother. I literally froze when I realised it was hers. I didn't have it saved, but I knew it was hers. Part of me wanted to ignore it while the other wanted to call her back. I wasn't sure if she knew what had transpired. I finally decided to call her back.

"Damn you, Danny," she said in a disappointed tone of voice. "I had such high hopes for you. All the paths you could have taken and you chose to waste your life selling numbers."

She sobbed quietly over the phone, so I knew she was really upset.

I had disappointed her so many times before, but she had never broken down like this.

"Please stop crying," I said.

"You have to give this shit up!" she shouted over the phone. "We're bringing you back home first thing tomorrow!"

"But you don't understand," I said. "Things are working out so well for me. I've worked too hard to give this all up. This is the best I've ever had life."

"This is the best you've had life," she said mockingly. "You're a damn fool! I hope they lock your ass up in jail and throw away the key! You'll learn then."

"I knew you wouldn't understand," I said.

"I swear to God if you are not back in the Creek by sundown tomorrow, I will come there and lick the shit out of you!" she threatened. "You young people will only learn when they put the handcuffs..."

I ended the call just like that. No goodbye, no call you later, no nothing. I will never forget that conversation as long as I live. That's how my mother was. She always said what was on her mind, and she didn't care how you felt about it. Charlene Bodden always did and said what the hell she wanted.

Afternoon turned to night. The apartment was quiet. Amanda was working the night shift. I was in the apartment all alone. The television was on but I paid little attention because I was so lost in my thoughts. There was a loud knock on the door which snapped me back to reality. Looking through the small peephole I saw nothing but darkness. Perhaps the bulb for the outside light had blown out. Foolish thinking.

I opened the apartment door slowly. A heavy-set guy pushed me to the floor with all his might. By the time I could get a sense of what was happening, someone grabbed me from behind. I was forced into a chair, and before I knew it, one of the other assailants was holding a pistol to my head.

"Give us your money!" he demanded. "Or I will pull this fucking trigger!"

I realised that I was being extorted.

"Where is it?" the second assailant bellowed.

"Where is what?" I answered back, pretending that I didn't have the faintest idea what he was referring to.

"You foo-foo awa?" the assailant with the pistol shouted. "Where's the Goddamn money! Give it to me before I blow your brains out!"

"My girlfriend's a police officer!" I shouted back, foolishly glancing at the phone, bringing attention to it.

"Grab the phone now!" the guy with the pistol instructed the other assailant.

I watched as he picked the cellphone up, walked outside and threw it from the second floor. A sharp thud could be heard as it hit the ground.

"You motherfuckers!" I shouted.

"Show us where it is!" the guy with the gun shouted, attempting to jab the head of the pistol right through my left temple.

I got up and walked to the bedroom, still at gunpoint, pulling out a small wad of cash out of the bottom nightstand drawer.

"This all you got?" he asked.

"Yes," I answered. "This is all I have! Don't kill me!"

Taking my word for it, the perpetrators vacated the premises immediately. It was a good thing that I kept most of my money in a cereal box at the far back of the pantry. I decided not to tell Amanda about what had happened – she surely would have insisted on a legitimate profession. When she returned from her shift later that night, I pretended to be asleep.

The next afternoon as I watched TV, Amanda at work, there was a knock at the door. I was reluctant to answer, obviously because of what happened the previous night. Looking through the peephole, there was my mother. I took a deep breath and opened the door slowly.

"Hello mother," I said, with a huge lump in my throat.

"Hello son," she said, clutching her large black handbag with both hands.

"How on earth did you find me?" I asked.

"Don't worry about that son," she said, taking a seat on one of the kitchen stools. "I need to get this off my chest."

"What is this about?" I questioned.

"Before you say anything else, you need to hear me out," she said. "I am not here to cuss and raise hell. You are your own man now. If this is the kind of young man you want to be, I won't stop you. But if for whatever reason things don't work out...if you ever want to come home...the door is always open."

"Dad didn't come?" I asked, using every ounce of strength I had to hold back my impending tears.

"This is killing him more than it's killing me," she said.

She walked out that door, and for the first time in a long time, I cried. Holding one of the sofa cushions, I literally curled up on the floor and the tears gushed out.

A few nights later, I was in the kitchen washing some dishes when there was a knock on the door. Through the peephole I could see that it was Amanda. I thought it strange that she didn't use her key, but I still opened the door for her. She entered the apartment slowly, two male police officers trailing right behind.

The three of them just looked at me.

"What the hell is this?" I finally blurted out, not making sense of the situation.

Abruptly, one of the officers cleared his throat loudly. He picked up my numbers book and float pouch off the dining room table.

"I'm afraid you'll have to come with us," he said, holding the paraphernalia.

"Why you dirty bitch!" I shouted to Amanda when it dawned on me.

"Guys, cuff him!" she instructed. "We've caught his ass red-handed."

Before I knew it, I was sitting in jail for the first time in my life. I was behind bars for two hours before I was let out for my one phone call. Every minute felt like an hour, and every hour a day. It literally made me sick to my stomach.

"We can let you go if you find someone who's willing to stand bail," the officer told me, grabbing me by the arm and roughly guiding me to the phone.

I decided to make that one phone call to Aunt Cecilia. Surely she would stand bail, despite kicking me out. But even she turned her back in my time of need. With that one phone call exhausted, the officer forcibly ushered me back to the cell. As I sat in that empty cell, alone, I had plenty of time to think. My thoughts turned to what had occurred over the last several months. I thought about how I had disappointed my family. I thought about how Amanda betrayed me. And lastly, I thought about how my life had now hit rock bottom.

But then, a breakthrough...

"You're free to go, son," the officer said. "Someone stood bail for you."

Assuming Aunt Cecilia had a change of heart, I exited the cell almost grinning. The officer grabbed my upper left arm firmly, looking at me menacingly.

"Your ass is not off the hook!" he said gruffly. "If I were you, I'd get myself a damn good lawyer."

As it turned out, Mr Lipton had stood bail.

"I owe you big time," I remember muttering to him.

"No charge," Mr Lipton replied, putting his hand on my shoulder. "I'm guessing you didn't smooth things over with your aunt."

"No, I didn't," I sighed. "She still doesn't want to talk to me."

"What about your parents?"

"I guess I'll have to swallow my pride," I said. "But how am I supposed to get back to them?"

"Don't worry about it, Danny," Mr. Lipton said, tapping my shoulder.

Back Home Again (#1)

The next morning I was on the Cayman Airways Saab aircraft heading back home to Cayman Brac. I walked the main road with one suitcase with some of Mr Lipton's old clothes. He gave me some of them because we had the same dress sizes and I couldn't collect mine from the apartment. No one was kind enough to offer a lift, so I had no choice but to walk until a good Samaritan picked me up and drove me to my parents' home. I took a deep sigh before knocking on the front door. After nearly a minute, my mother answered.

"Why I can't believe it!" she said, giving me a hug.

The house hadn't changed one bit. All my baby pictures and graduation portraits were displayed proudly around the living room.

"I think you should sit down," I urged, gently weaselling out of the hug.

"What is it?" she questioned with a concerned tone.

"I will tell you as soon as you sit down," I urged again.

Slowly, my mother sat down on the couch.

"Listen, I've gotten into a little trouble," I said rubbing the crown of my head.

"How much trouble?" she asked.

"They caught me red handed," I said. "I had to spend the night in jail."

"I figured that would happen sooner or later," she said. "But of course you young people think you have the PhD before you even start the courses."

"But I got bailed out," I said.

"I can see that," she said sarcastically. "Who bailed you out may I ask?"

"You don't know him," I said, thinking that she didn't know Mr. Lipton.

"Who bailed you out!" she insisted.

"If you must know, his name is Mr. Lipton."

"Oh dear God!" she said. "I hope you don't mean James Anthony Lipton?"

"Yes," I confirmed.

"You have no idea who you're dealing with!" she warned me. "You need to stay away from that man!"

"At least he bailed me out!" I said. "Aunt Cecilia didn't!"

"You leave your Aunt Cecilia out of this!" she shouted. "If you only knew what you put that poor woman through! I don't trust Lipton at all! And don't expect us to bail you out. You got yourself in this mess and you will get your ass out."

I darted into my bedroom, Mom following behind.

"I want my son back!" she shouted before heading back into the living room.

I walked out with my suitcase, using the last of the money that Mr Lipton had given me to get buy a one-way ticket back to Grand Cayman. Mr Lipton was stumbling down the stairs from the second-floor airport bar when I returned.

"Things didn't work out huh?"

"No," I said.

"Let's go," Mr Lipton slurred.

Once more I walked up Mr Lipton's rickety set of stairs to the spare bedroom. I laid in bed trying to take a nap as the sun was setting. It was dark outside by the time I woke up. The whole house was in darkness as usual. I found Mr Lipton on the back porch, clutching a glass of Amaretto.

"You alright, Mr. Lipton?" I asked.

"I'm alright," he replied, as I sat down next to him.

"This whole situation going on with you right now reminds me of when I was growing up," he said. "I was a rebel in those days. I remember sneaking out one night to see my girlfriend. I was about fifteen then."

"You were a rebel from then," I remarked.

"You bet!" he laughed. "Anyway, when I came back home my mother was there waiting. She told me to take off my belt 'cause she was gonna beat the shit out of me. But little did she know."

"What did you do?" anxious to find out how he avoided her wrath.

"I took off the belt and gave it to her. She attempted to beat me but I managed to grab the belt and pulled her forward. I looked her dead in her eyes and told her 'my beating days are fucking over'."

"And what did she say?"

"She was too shocked to say anything," I said. "She wasn't expecting that I guess. And I was so much bigger than her by that point."

"What happened after that?"

"I ended up going to sea not too long after," he said. "Worked on a freightliner called the Caldeman. She was a massive vessel, one of the biggest ships in the world at that time."

"Wait a minute," I blurted. "Did you say the Caldeman?"

"Yeah, why?"

"My father used to work on the Caldeman," I said. "He was one of the cooks."

"You know, one of my exes ended up marrying a cook that worked on that ship," he said. "Her name was Charlene."

"Wait a minute," I said. "My mother's name is Charlene."

"She's your mother?" he said lighting up. "The one that got away! I was gonna propose to her. But then she broke it off. Said that she couldn't be with me anymore; she didn't explain why and it's not that I didn't ask. But I guess it wasn't meant to be. My God, I haven't seen her since."

I couldn't understand why my mother spoke so ill of the man. After all, it seemed that he really loved her. Anyway, when Mr. Lipton left the next morning, I flicked through a book on the kitchen counter when a newspaper clipping dropped out. It was precisely that newspaper clipping that enlightened me to the fact that Mr. Lipton may not be the nice, down-on-his-luck man that he was trying to make me believe he was.

James Anthony Lipton, 40, appeared in court today in connection with the murder of Barbara Martin...A letter from an unidentified woman who allegedly witnessed the murder from a nearby building, which some anonymous sources claimed was an ex-partner of the defendant and a cousin of Ms. Martin, was presented as evidence in court...

Then it dawned on me why my mother despised Mr. Lipton. I remember her saying once that her first cousin, Barbara, was killed in a tragic accident. From this clipping, it seemed as if Mr. Lipton was responsible for the death of my family member. How the hell could I respect a man who did something like that?

But I wasn't in a position to leave until weeks later. However, I wasn't moving on to a better place. I was sentenced to twelve months imprisonment at H.M. Northward Prison, which I served unwillingly. After my release, I made up my mind to return home to Cayman Brac for good. Mr. Lipton paid for the ticket and I returned to the island as an ex-convict. I was grateful for what Mr. Lipton had done, but with ninety miles of sea separating us, I would be washing my hands of him for good.

I spent the night in my own bedroom for the first time in months. I ate breakfast at the old dining table; corned beef with white rice, but as far as I was concerned it was fillet mignon. That afternoon, when my parents and I went to buy groceries, I ran into one of my former classmates, Elias.

"Ole boy, is that you?" he asked, as he smoked a cigarette.

During our last year of high school, he was sent off to Canada to military school and I hadn't seen him since.

"My God," I said. "I haven't seen you since you went off to Canada!"

"I know, right," he said. "So how have things been?"

"I don't even know where to begin," I said. "My life is so screwed up."

"Yeah, mine too," he said.

"What are you doing back here?"

"I got kicked out of military school," he said. "It was the toughest military school in Canada. They practically begged my Dad to fly up there and get me."

"So what are you doing with yourself now?"

"I'm working in the family business," he said. "I do a little bit of everything, and they give me a couple of dollars every week."

"That's good," I remarked.

"So what you been doing with yourself?" he asked, throwing what was left of the cigarette on the ground.

"I just got out of Northward," I said.

"You serious?"

"Serious as a judge," I said. "You can ask my parents. I was in there for a year. Got caught selling numbers. I just got out actually."

"That's hardcore still," he said. "So, what brings you down this way?"

"My parents came to do some shopping," I said. "Then we're heading back."

"Listen, buddy, I have a little errand to run later tonight," as Elias innocently put it. "You can come along if you want."

"Yeah sure, I'll come along," I said, having no idea what I was agreeing to.

"I'll come by the house around three," he said. "You'll be ready right?"

We exchanged phone numbers, but I took it with a grain of salt.

My First Career

I was fast asleep when the loud vibration of my cellphone woke me up. It was Elias calling, letting me know that he was waiting outside.

"We'd better get going," he said.

He was dressed in full black. His face was covered, with the exception of his eyes, nose and mouth. I thought it strange that he was dressed like that. But then it dawned on me; he was getting ready to commit a robbery.

"Why the hell are you dressed like that?" I blurted.

"We gotta do what we gotta do," he said.

"But I can't do this!" I said. "I can't go back to Northward!"

The last thing on my mind was committing a robbery. But against my better judgement, I quickly went back inside and dressed in dark clothing as well. We parked on a deserted trail, walking through a shortcut that led to the back of a jewellery store (I'm not saying which one for obvious reasons). With the help of a lock-picking kit, Elias managed to gain entry through the back door open. We ransacked the whole store trying to find anything of value, but no to avail.

Trying our luck in the back storeroom, I accidentally brushed up against some empty boxes stacked on top of one another. As they tumbled to the ground, I realised that my clumsiness revealed something of value. A carpet bag fell out of one of the boxes, and fortuitously for us, it was full of money.

We headed home through the darkness to count the loot, Elias securing the loot in his bedroom. The next day the robbery was the talk of the town.

I watched from a distance later that morning, trying to be discreet. The owner of the jewellery store sobbed uncontrollably outside as a uniformed police officer jotted notes down in a small pocket notepad. As the owner managed a word or two between sobs, I watched discreetly from a distance as a crowd slowly gathered.

"What am I going to do?" she moaned. "I'm ruined!"

"Don't you worry," the officer said, placing the notepad back into his pocket. "We'll find the bastards and we'll find every last penny!"

The next night Elias had dressed in full black again. He would be committing another robbery and I would reprise my role as his accomplice. Quickly dressing in 'robbery attire' we broke into a liquor store, in the same vicinity of the same jewellery store. Although the police promised to beef up patrols around the area, I was surprised to see that they hadn't. Elias headed straight for the storeroom and we found cash. He stuffed the money into his backpack, while I grabbed two big bottles of spiced rum and a carton of cigarettes.

Within weeks we committed several more robberies, amassing over eleven thousand dollars. By this point, I thought we had stolen more than enough. We would be pushing our luck if we attempted any more. I thought it was best to take a break, at least until everything blew over. Elias and I had progressed so far with our life of crime without getting caught. No one had suspected us of the robberies, which was remarkable. But I had had enough of stealing. Desiring to earn some honest dollars for a change, I wanted to pull out from the partnership altogether.

I woke up to my mother sobbing over breakfast, hoping that she hadn't found out about my involvement in the break-ins. I had hurt her enough and if she found this out, it would probably kill her.

"What happened?" I asked, putting her hands on her shoulders.

"I've given your father our last couple of dollars to get some groceries," she said. "He should be back any minute now."

I gave a sigh of relief in a sense.

"But why are you crying?"

"I don't think your father's gonna be able to go back to work," she said. "I don't know what's going to happen to us. He's nearing retirement age, and I don't know what Public Works is going to do with him."

"Why do you say that?" I asked.

"Have you looked at him? The poor man can barely stand up straight. He's been hunched over for months."

I couldn't tell her about all the money I had stolen. Elias and I had split the money equally, and I had nearly six thousand dollars hidden in one of my bureau drawers. We had money in the house, only that I couldn't tell anyone.

"I think we need we need to cool out on the stealing," I finally plucked up the courage to tell Elias. "We have more than enough to get by for quite a while."

"You coming with this shit again!" Elias shouted, annoyed that I was mentioning it to him again

"Look...I can't do this anymore!" I asserted. "Do whatever you want."

I got off of Elias's couch and walked towards the foyer.

"Where the hell are you going?" Elias shouted.

I didn't respond. I hit the road and hitched a ride with some tourists. They let me off at Ann Tatum Road which ran past my house. There was a trail of some sort between the road and Ebenezer Baptist Church, which I walked through. I stood before the church I was raised in, seeing parishioners entering the church for Wednesday night service. I knew practically all of them but none said a word to me; perhaps they had all heard about my plight. I wanted to enter, but was reluctant to because I wasn't dressed in church clothes. Then an elderly lady walking with a cane appeared, whom I didn't know.

"Where you headed, son?" she asked.

"I don't know," I said, rubbing the back of my head with my hand.

"Well, if you don't have anywhere special to go," she said. "You're more than welcome to join us for worship."

"Thank you," I said. "But I'm not dressed."

"God says come as you are," she reminded me with a sweet smile.

I do believe that God sent her to me to get me into the church that night because I never saw her again. I sheepishly took a seat at the back pew, feeling like a fish out of water. However, this night paved the way for the new path I would take in life. Within a year's time, Elias's days of criminal activity had come to a crushing end. He ended up getting caught with cocaine in Little Cayman and was sent to prison. Fortunately for me, I left the partnership before everything went south.

My Second Career

I was raking leaves one afternoon when my father came out to me.
"Lunch is ready," he announced.
This afternoon we were eating stewed beef with steamed vegetables and Spanish rice, which one of my mother's crocheting buddies had cooked and brought for us. We were ashamed that practically everyone in the neighborhood knew of our financial plight, but it was the first decent meal we had eaten in days.

"At least we managed to pay off the house," my father announced over dinner. "We sold that piece of land at the right time. If we didn't have that piece of land to sell then we would really be in a mess today!"

"I told you that piece of land would come in handy eventually," my mother said with a huge smirk on her face. "We pinched pennies for about six years to pay for it. But guess what? It saved our house. And you thought it was a waste of money."

"You heard anything from the liquor store yet?" my father asked my mother, diverting the conversation. He didn't need to be reminded that the land purchase was against his will.

"Not a thing," she said. "Hopefully they'll call soon. You found anything?"

"Nope nothing for me either," he said. "What about you, Danny?"

"I haven't found anything either," I said.

"Tell you the truth son," he said. "If you could get into the fire service now, we'd be sort of okay."

Those were the words I had wanted to hear from my father my whole life. Unfortunately, my chances of getting into the fire service now were next to nothing.

"It's only by the grace of God we've made it this long," my father said. "All I can tell you…if you see anything for the fire service in the paper, try for it."

"The end of the month is coming up and we've got bills coming our way again." my mother said. "And we don't have a red cent to pay them with."

She quickly grabbed for her purse while my father and I grabbed for our wallets. I pulled out a ten dollar note while my father pulled out a crumpled twenty-five dollar note, and my mother pulled out a crisp fifty dollar note.

"This is pitiful," my father said, totally discouraged.

Then the idea hit me. It was perfect! Why did I not think of that before?

"Let's have a yard sale!" I suddenly announced. "We can break this money into smaller bills for float!"

"What the hell do we have in this house to sell?" he said.

"Look around!" I said. "We've got a house full of stuff that we don't even use! For example, look at this China cabinet. Everything in there is just gathering dust."

"I am not selling my china!" Mom said. "Don't even think about it!"

"But the china is no good to us if we don't use it," I said, trying to reason with her. "We don't even use it for Christmas anymore."

"Alright, fine," said my mother, resigned.

We held our yard sale a few days later that Saturday, making about five hundred dollars. Shortly thereafter, we all secured work in the community clean-up programme and waited every Friday afternoon for our cheques.

Eventually, after months of working in the community clean-up programme, I managed to land a gardening job with a politician in George Town. The pay wasn't that great, just three hundred dollars a week, but I could live in a small studio apartment behind his house for free.

"You gotta do what you gotta do," my father said after I had announced the news. "We'll miss you but you'll have to make a steady living somehow."

"Yes child," my mother reinforced. "You have your whole life ahead of you."

"What's gonna happen to you guys?" I asked.

"Don't worry about us," my father said. "We'll survive. We always do."

I remember the day I left, an overcast Sunday morning. By the time I arrived in George Town, someone at the airport was already waiting for me in a Mercedes Benz S 550. For the entire fifteen minute drive the driver remained silent; I don't think he spoke English that well. As we pulled up to the politician's house, I could see a huge sign erected by the gate. It had a photo of the man with large lettering underneath which simply said *'Elect Kenneth Archer on 24 May'*.

It was an overcast day as the Mercedes Benz drove down a long paved driveway that led to a three-car garage behind the house, the studio apartment located adjacent in a detached structure. As I was unpacking there was a knock at the door. I thought it was the driver from earlier, but surprisingly it was Mr. Archer.

"So you're the young man from the Brac that I hired," he said, shaking my hand firmly. It was a little stronger than I had expected, definitely no limp greeting.

"Yes sir," I replied. "Not too much longer until the election, eh?"

"The time is really creeping up on me," he said. "It's just three weeks from today. Listen, I'm actually having a meeting in the front yard tomorrow night, so I'll need you to clean up around there."

"No problem sir," I said. "It's my job isn't it?"

"I like that enthusiasm!" he said, placing his hand on my shoulder. "I need to finish up my speech for tomorrow, so I have to go. Ahhh, the life of a politician."

"I can imagine sir," I said.

At sunrise the next morning, I got straight to work. There were lots to get done in time for the meeting so the earlier the better. I was almost finished trimming some hedges that grew behind the front gate when Mr. Archer walked out the front door. Dressed in a light blue dress shirt and a red tie, probably to remain neutral to party lines, he clutched his briefcase as he walked towards me.

"I need you to give it one hundred percent today," he said. "I have to make a good impression."

I watched as he drove his 2013 Mercedes-Benz S 550 onto the road this time. He also owned a 1990 Ford F150 truck and a 1992 Mercedes-Benz S 420, hence the need for a three-car garage.

Mr Archer was the long-serving member of the Cayman Islands Legislative Assembly for the district of George Town. He had done remarkably well for someone who dropped out of high school at fourteen. He persevered in spite of obstacles, having run two unsuccessful campaigns before winning the trust of his constituents.

I would learn later that Mr. Archer was raised by a single mother who earned meagre wages as a hotel housekeeper.

This was in the early days of Caymanian tourism, long before Caymankind but when it had a very Caymanian face. Raised in the face of near poverty, with the lack of a father figure and an incomplete education, he still became successful.

However, for the 2017 general elections, the George Town district had now become splintered into six. He now found himself running in the newly-formed district of George Town Central. Each of the six districts required only one member to represent them; known as single-member constituencies. This is the case with all other multi-member constituencies of the Cayman Islands except East End and North Side, which were single-member constituencies to begin with.

I sensed that Mr. Archer was nervous about the impending election. Perhaps he was worried about losing his seat to younger and more educated candidates. However, straw polls in the various newspapers gave him a tremendous lead over his opponents. He had the most political experience out of anyone in the race.

By the time the meeting started that evening, the yard was packed. At seven o'clock sharp, Mr. Archer exited his front door and walked up to the makeshift stage to address the enthusiastic crowd.

The Election Campaign

"My friends, it is that time again!" he shouted over the microphone. "It is the Big E! Election time! I trust that when you go to the polls on the 24th of May you will make the right choice! You need to vote for a candidate who is experienced, someone who has produced tangible results for this district, someone who has integrity and vision! That individual is none other than myself!"

The crowd clapped and hollered loudly.

"My friends, we have achieved so much these past four years," he bellowed. "A lot of the work has been done quietly because I am not a person to brag, but we still have a ways to go. With your help, I will ensure that everything I set out to do is completed and completed well!"

The crowd clapped and hollered loudly again.

"Too many of our kids are still going to school hungry," he said. "Too many of our people can't keep the lights on, can't get the rent paid, can't get the mortgage paid. But I have done everything in my power to ensure that progress has been made. I have tried my best to keep in touch with, you, my constituents. It was a priority of mine to keep everyone abreast of the business of the Legislative Assembly, whether I had your support or not!"

The crowd clapped and hollered loudly.

After a spirited campaign meeting, dozens and dozens of supporters began partaking of refreshments. They each left the yard with a brightly coloured campaign t-shirt to proclaim their alliance. I joined the food table sheepishly, picking up a tiny foam plate. The server placed one chicken wing, one fish filet and one tiny piece of light cake onto it.

I sat in one of the chairs in the back row and ate quietly. I watched as Mr Archer played the crowd, eventually meandering towards me.

"You enjoyed the meeting?" he asked.

"Yes sir, I did," even though I thought it was all rhetoric.

"I didn't look too nervous did I?"

"No sir, not at all," I assured him.

"I was shaking like a leaf," he admitted. "I'm glad it didn't show. Listen, you don't have to stick around if you don't want. Get some more food and head back to the apartment."

I got another plate of food and did as I was told.

Mr Archer continued to have meetings throughout the district and visit people in their homes and businesses, trying to keep his seat.

The big day arrived quickly; Election Day. It was a public holiday and Mr Archer gave me the day off. However, the election was not important to me as I was not registered to vote yet. The day wore on. I found two large boxes of books inside the pantry, and I spent the entire day reading. It was the first time I had read a book from cover to cover in months.

At five o'clock that afternoon I decided to turn on the radio to hear what was going on with the elections. Even though I couldn't vote, I still found it exciting. Besides, there wasn't much else to do and my job security may have depended upon Mr. Archer's re-election.

"Hello and thank you for tuning in to our coverage of...*crackling*...general elections. It is now approximately one hour until the polls officially close so if you haven't voted please try to get to the polls as quickly as possible."

I tuned in to another station.

"I am standing just outside the exclusion zone at one of the polling stations at West Bay North and there is still a huge crowd here still waiting to vote. However people seem to be coming in and out quite swiftly."

I listened for several minutes before taking a quick stroll around the yard. The neighbourhood was quiet. Families were settled inside listening to election updates.

"It is now seven minutes past the hour of six o'clock and the polls are officially closed. As we speak elections officials are getting the ballot boxes ready to be delivered to the designated counting stations across the nation. *crackling* We now have the latest news from the election command centre in the capital George Town. The Elections Supervisor has just stated that the turnout for the total electorate is 70.34%, the lowest turnout since the 1996 general elections."

I decided to leave the yard and take a walk around the neighbourhood, as dusk was setting in. Past the security of those white gates, all I could hear was the faint sound of election news from the houses nearby. People were huddled in living rooms and bedrooms listening in. An older man was sitting on the steps that led to his small home listening to his portable radio.

The night rolled in. I awoke minutes to midnight tuning in to hear the results.

"Ladies and gentlemen...*crackling*...the votes for George Town Central are about 97% counted now and long-time candidate Kenneth Archer appears to be taking a small lead... *crackling*...It seems as if Kenneth Archer is going to keep his seat yet again!"

This latest update was to be followed by more crackling.

"Hello and welcome back to our special election coverage! We will turn now to our...*crackling* in George Town Central. Hello are you there?"

"Yes I am here. The station supervisor has now come from outside the building and is now going to formally announce who will become the elected member for George Town Central."

I could hear as one of the elections supervisors began to speak.

"I would like to say thank you to our elections officials who have spent a lot of time away from their families these last few months in preparation for election day and for maintaining law and order today. I can say that we have had a smooth elections process this year, for George Town Central at least."

There was a loud beeping noise for several seconds.

"Now let's get on to our results. We have #1 Kenneth Moses Archer with 462 votes, #2 Nicholas Angelo Berry with 97 votes and #3 Paul Alden Tyson with 207 votes. Therefore, Kenneth Moses Archer is the elected member for Marburn Town East until the next election cycle in 2021."

I could hear the sound of applause and people cheering. I turned the radio off and took another snooze. When I awoke, I saw Mr. Archer trying to unlock the back door. I went outside to congratulate him.

"Oh Danny, it's you," he said as he let out a huge yawn, stretched a little, and took a quick glance at his gold wristwatch.

"Congrats, Mr. Archer!" I said, shaking his hand.

"Thank you son," he said yawning again. "Boy I'm tired! I'm gonna drink a little glass of Merlot and go to bed. Would you care for some?"

"Yes sir," I said, not particularly caring for Merlot, but acquiescing out of respect. I didn't want to turn down this esteemed gentleman's offer.

This was the first time I ever entered the main house. I entered through the back door, which led straight into the kitchen. I was shocked to see how dated the kitchen was, given the handsome remuneration that this man received. But I digress. I watched as he poured the Merlot into two wide mouthed wine glasses. I took a tiny sip, pretending to like it.

"Well, I've survived another election," he said as he took a sip. "But I think that this will be my last term."

"Why?" I asked.

"I've been in this game long enough," he said. "Time to pass the reins onto the younger generation. I was gonna retire this year but I got calls from so many people to run again and I couldn't say no. But I do believe this is the final curtain call."

"What do you plan to do when you retire?" I asked. "Won't you be bored?"

"Son, when you get to be my age, you look forward to boredom," he said. "I've barely had time to piss for a very long time. I'm gonna catch up on my reading, go for long walks on the beach. I've got seven acres of farmland behind this house and I'm gonna plant off every damn square inch of it! I bought that ground in 1990 and I always tell myself that I was gonna start a farm, grow what I eat. Imagine twenty seven years on, I still haven't done a damn thing!"

The Late Mr. Archer

Just over an hour later, after a few drinks, Mr. Archer retired upstairs to get some much-needed rest. I went back to the apartment to do the same. A week later, Mr. Archer was sworn in and continued with his work as an MLA. I continued with my daily work, and we would get together once every couple of weeks for a drink or two.

Mr. Archer had so many plans for the country, but like my mother used to say *'you don't plan for life, life plans for you'*

It made the front page of the newspaper. My heart sank when I saw it.

'Political stalwart Kenneth Archer dies at 63'

I read the first few sentences of the article, still hardly believing it:

"The Hon. Kenneth Archer, a current and long-standing political stalwart of the Cayman Islands has passed away, aged 63. Archer passed away at the Cayman Islands Hospital last night from an apparent heart attack...He leaves behind one son,

Nathaniel and three grandchildren."

The paper was dated Wednesday 26 July 2017, two months and two days after the election. I couldn't come to terms with the fact that Mr. Archer had passed away. But most importantly, and a little selfishly; did I still have a job?

I exited the apartment. The place seemed desolate. Then I saw a woman come out from the back door with a garbage bag in hand.

"Who are you?" I asked.

"Who the hell are you?" she rudely retorted.

"I'm Danny, his gardener," I replied.

She gave out a huge sigh.

"If you must know, I'm Shannon," she said, probably realising that she may have been a bit brash. "I'm his housekeeper"

"I've never seen you before," I said.

"And I've never seen you," she said. "How long have you been the gardener?"

"Three months."

"I've been here for five months," she said. "I got laid off from the hotel I was working at and Mr. Archer took me on as his housekeeper until I can find a new job. It's only three days a week but it's better than nothing. I guess you heard about Mr. Archer," she asked me.

"Yeah, I just read about it in the paper," I said.

"Frankly, I'm not surprised," she said. "I didn't see him eat a single vegetable, at least since I've been working here. Every afternoon when he came in, it was fried chicken or bacon and eggs, glasses of whiskey and vodka. This was day in, day out. He was a heart attack waiting to happen."

"I just can't get over it," I said. "We had a drink of whiskey just the other night, right there in the kitchen. You know what, now that I think about it, he was complaining about this pressure in his chest, and when he was climbing the stairs he said that he had felt dizzy."

"I noticed that too," she said. "He was complaining about the same thing. I had to help him up the stairs the other day."

"What are we gonna do?" I asked. "How are we gonna get paid?"

"I don't know," she sighed.

A few days later I returned from grocery shopping to find an eviction notice and a plain white envelope taped to the door. Inside the envelope was a cheque made out to me for three hundred dollars, my last paycheque. It was one of Nathaniel Archer's cheques to be exact.

Shannon exited from the main house as I thoughtfully closed the envelope.

"He's sending his secretary to get our stuff out in a few minutes," she said.

"But he shouldn't kick us out just like that!" I said.

"I guess he doesn't see it that way," she said. "Did you get a cheque too?"

"Yep, five hundred dollars," I answered.

"We got the same amount then," she said.

We waited around until Nathaniel's uptight secretary arrived, wearing a dark grey pants suit and a pair of black high heels she could barely walk in. Taking a huge bundle of keys from her shiny Michael Kors handbag, she opened the door for Shannon to enter the main house and then opened the door to my apartment.

"Hurry up and get your stuff out!" she said in annoyed tone. "I've got plenty to do and so little time!"

It only took about fifteen minutes to hurriedly pack my things into two tattered suitcases. I left the apartment to find the secretary standing with her arms folded.

"It's about time." she said, rather annoyed.

Shannon and I went our separate ways, cashing my cheque just before the bank closed. I bought a plane ticket, rented a hotel room for the night and headed for the airport the next morning.

I was heading home to Cayman Brac once again.

Back Home Again (#2)

The plane landed on the runway in West End, and once again I was back home. After a long conversation about what had transpired over the past few months, my father went out to do some errands. After a few hours, my mother thought that he was taking a bit long but figured he would pop through the door as usual, smelling like a mix of piped tobacco and Ted Lapidus.

Mother's cellphone vibrated loudly on the kitchen counter.

"Hello," she said. "Yes, this is Ralph's wife...oh Christ not again! I'll get someone to pick him up...yes thanks!"

"What is it?" I asked.

"Ummm...It's that father of yours," she said looking at the floor. "He's at La Esperanza inside bar, drunk as a coot. He probably ran into those work buddies of his along the way. But knowing him he probably got all the errands done before he started drinking. Anyway, I need you to pick him up."

"But I don't even have my licence."

"You never worried about it before," she said.

With that said, I drove about a mile down the road to La Esperanza and walked inside the bar. There was my father seated in the corner.

"Get me away from all these drunk people!" he ordered with a heavy tongue.

I helped him out of the chair and managed to get him into the car. As I drove, it dawned on me how much weight he had lost. He was almost skin and bone. When we got home he began to vomit profusely outside the house.

"Oh sweet Jesus!" Mother shouted from inside the house. "Try to get him to the backyard before the neighbours see."

It was too late. I already eyed one of them, pretending to trim the hedges.

"Nosy bitch," I thought to myself.

He finished throwing up in the backyard before I helped him through the back door, planning to get him to the master bedroom to sleep off his impending hangover.

"I'm not making your father sleep in the bedroom like that!" she said sternly. "I just put on the new bedsheets!"

"Where is he supposed to go?" I questioned.

"There's a clean tarpaulin in the shed," she said quickly. "Lay it out in the laundry room and I'll find an old pillow for him to rest his head on."

"I'm not making my father sleep on a tarpaulin!" I retorted.

"With the way I feel these days, you should be happy that you're not lying alongside him!" she snapped.

At first I was offended, but then I realised why she was speaking like that. She was so fed up with his drinking, it was a wonder she hadn't just walked out on us. I did as I was told. He laid right there on that blue tarpaulin, knocked out cold.

"If he wants to act like a dog, we'll treat him like a damn dog!" my mother said. You have no idea what I've gone through since you left!"

"You mean this is a regular thing?"

"Very much so," she confirmed. "Every other day he drinks himself into a stupor. I can't believe my life has come to this!"

She walked slowly towards the back door, walking over my father like he was garbage. He didn't even stir.

"I'm tired Goddamnit!" Mom shouted at the top of her lungs. "If I wasn't so devoted, if I wasn't such a good person I would've walked out long time!"

I hugged her tightly as she sobbed in frustration. Arm around her, we walked inside, hoping to cool down.

The next day as I ate breakfast, Dad appeared looking like death.

"Christ I feel horrible!" he said, dragging his feet along the linoleum floor. "Honey get me some aspirin and a gun to blow my brains out."

"You deserve what you get!" she said, obediently bringing water and aspirin.

I noticed yesterday's newspaper on the counter. Picking it up and turning straight to the employment section, I wished there was some job that I could get, even if it was picking up garbage on the side of the road."

And then I found the perfect advert, like it was there waiting for me to find it!

"The Periwinkle Soda Co. Ltd. is seeking workers for their Cayman Brac plant...$6.50 an hour...no experience necessary."

I walked down to their office the next day and picked up an application form. By the time I arrived back home, my father had long fell asleep at the kitchen table. As my mother tiptoed across the room, I wondered why the hell she was doing that.

"I just got off the phone with the doctor," she said whispering. "She wants your father to come to the hospital tomorrow morning for a check up."

"Doesn't he get those all the time?" I said, not understanding why she had to whisper that and tiptoe around the damn living room.

"This checkup is very, very important," she stressed. "This one determines whether or not your father can go back to work. He's been on half-pay all this time, and we could barely make it with his full pay cheque."

"But they can't just fire him," I said. "Worst case scenario, they'll have to retire him on medical."

"Don't make me laugh!" she said. "Your Dad's only gonna get six hundred and seventy five dollars and month...and how are we gonna survive off that? Your father can drink that out in two days."

My Third Career

I began my first day at Periwinkle on a Monday morning, with the news that my father was returning to work within the next few weeks. The Quality Control Supervisor, who was addressed and referred to as Hopkins, was widely disliked by the other workers due to his moodiness and sarcasm. Surprisingly, I was the only line worker who got along with him. He was actually so impressed by my performance that he tasked me with training all the new workers that came along. I sensed that everyone was jealous of this, but it didn't matter to me.

Jeanette was the only line worker that I was close with. We clicked from day one, and she was my only confidant at work, in spite of being twenty six years older than me. We often went out for drinks after work, which only fueled rumours within the workplace that I was having an affair with Jeanette. But that was not the case at all. I regarded Jeanette as an aunt in a sense, and I felt that could tell her anything without being judged.

And then Kimberly came into the picture.

She initially came on during the Christmas rush as a seasonal worker, from the first week of December to the second week of January. I thought she was attractive and considered asking her out on a date; however, I decided against it because we were in the same department. But I do remember sitting together at the Christmas party complaining about how boring it was. However, I did find out some valuable information there.

I remember her telling me that she had an Associates Degree in Business Administration from the University College of the Cayman Islands. I knew that one of the office assistants would be leaving on 31 December, and that the job would become available. Sure enough, the new year rolled in and Kimberly's contract ended. At my urging, she applied and got the office assistant job about a month later. With Kimberly now in a different department, I decided to give it a shot.
"What do you have for lunch today?" she asked that Monday afternoon. She always asked the same thing.
"Just this sandwich and this juice box." I answered, showing her the brown paper bag it was in. "What about you?"
"Some curry chicken from last night," she said.
Then finally I came out with it.
"Listen, if you're not doing anything special this weekend, maybe we could go out for a drink."
She just stared at me, kinda stunned.
"Are you asking me what I think you're asking me?"
There was a very brief but awkward pause.
"Yes," I replied.
There was another very brief but awkward pause.
"Why the hell not," she replied. "Let me give you my number."

We both rendezvoused at La Esperanza, walking there from my house. I would find out that she didn't have a driver's licence either. I bought her a drink and we sat by the seaside bar. We talked for a long time watching the water lap up against the support posts of the pier.
Her father lived in Miami, and they hadn't seen each other in about four years. Her mother was in and out of Fairbanks prison, her

mother actually in again for theft and criminal trespass. However, she was stealing with good intentions, trying to ensure that her bills could be paid and her children could have the best. Kimberly lived about a quarter mile from my house with her sister Leanna. They had just rented a small two-bedroom house.

When the bar closed, Kimberly and I weren't ready to part, so I decided to bring her back to my room. Sneaking her into the house, we would make love for the first time. I was glad that I could take her virginity in a place where I felt comfortable. As we lay there naked, only covered by a sheet, I woke up and realised that it was eight o'clock. She was to leave just before dawn, but we didn't wake up in time.

"Shit, we overslept!" I whispered to her, trying to gently nudge her.

"Oh hell!" she blurted.

She quickly slipped into her dress and tried to exit the bedroom. With the bougainvillea now trimmed, this was made a little easier. She quickly slipped her small frame through the window and left.

Our romance continued. Over the next several months, I assumed that my parents were unaware of the relationship. Little did I know...

"How come you didn't tell me about your friend?" my mother asked that afternoon, as I came home from work.

"What are you talking about?"

"The friend that I saw coming out of your bedroom window a few months ago," she said. "Does that ring a bell dear?"

The cat was out of the bag. I didn't say a word, which annoyed her.

"I wanna meet this girl!" she said.

"What are you shouting about out there?" Dad yelled from the bedroom.

"Come out here Ralph!" she shouted back. "This son of mine has a girlfriend that he hasn't told us about yet!"

He came out almost running.

"Really?" he said, like a little boy in a candy store.

"Yes, he had her over here a few months ago," she reiterated. "In his bedroom, he must have brought her over for the night."

My father's face broke out into a grin, the opposite of what I had expected.

"You don't think this is okay, do you?" she said to him.

"Look Charlene, I don't agree with the whole bringing a woman here at night thing," he clarified. "But I am glad that he found someone."

"Anyway," she said. "I wanna meet this girl. Ask her when she can come over and I'll cook a lovely meal. Do you agree Ralph?"

"I wouldn't mind that," he said.

"Oh for goodness sake!" I blurted, being very careful to say 'goodness' instead of 'Christ'. Though my mother would occasionally curse, Christ was off limits.

"I will ask her."

The next day during my water break I went to the office to see Kimberly.

"What's up?" I asked her.

"Plenty of work today," she said, pointing at the stack of papers around her.

"Listen Kimberly," I said. "My parents wanna meet you. They want you to come over for dinner one night."

"Wait a minute, how did your parents know?" she questioned. "Who blabbed up inside here. No one here is supposed to know!"

"Shhh!" I said, putting my hand on her shoulder. "My mother saw you sneaking out of my bedroom window some months ago."

"Oh," she said. "So no one here knows?"

"I don't think so," I said. "So will you come please?"

"I'm not good at meeting parents," she said.

"Please, you only have to come for an hour," I pleaded. "Then you can make up some excuse that you have to be somewhere."

"Alright fine!" she said. "I'll come tomorrow night, but if I don't like how things are going, I will leave in an hour!"

Tomorrow night rolled around and Kimberly arrived right on time. Mother was wearing her oversized emerald green dress with a pair of slingbacks.

"Any excuse to wear that damn dress", I thought to myself.

But surprisingly we had a good time. Kimberly ended up staying two hours longer than planned.

"You know what?" Mom said. "I like that girl."

"She's alright," said Father.

I was surprised that they liked her, even though I had snuck her into the house and had sexual intercourse with her. Time continued to pass, and our relationship developed further.

I should have known something was up. Why the hell would she ask me to meet her by the dumpsters after work? I wanted her to tell me the news over the phone. However, she insisted that she wanted to tell me in person.

"Babe, there's something I need to tell you," she said.

"Well what is it?" I asked. "You could've told me over the phone."

"I'm pregnant," she blurted.

"Are you sure?" I asked.

She opened her handbag; all it contained was three used pregnancy tests, all positive. Now I wasn't ready for a child; I was only twenty-three. But I just couldn't stomach the idea of Kimberly having an abortion. I had to ask.

"Do you want to keep it?" I queried, half-expecting her to say no.

"Honestly, I'm not ready for a child," she said. "But I'm keeping it."

We hugged each other tightly, basically all we could do. The only thing left to do was to tell my parents.

"I'm going to be a Dad," I blurted over Sunday lunch, four days after, finally building up the courage to tell them.

"Are you sure?" my mother asked.

"Kimberly took three pregnancy tests, and they were all positive," I said.

Surprisingly they were pretty cool about it, almost excited in fact. They did tell me the usual stuff that parents would say; that having a child was a big responsibility, etcetera. They wished that I waited a few years more and that I was married, but they seemed happy to have a grandchild coming nonetheless.

Seven months later, because she was about two months pregnant when she told me, our son Ronaldo was born 5lbs, 4oz. When I held Renaldo for the first time, I knew that my life had changed forever.

References

Whittaker, James (23 October 2015). 'Church raffles legalized in Gambling Law change'.
Retrieved from: https://www.caymancompass.com/2015/10/23/church-raffles-legalized-in-gambling-law-change/

Winker, Carol (10 August 2011). Woman fined for selling numbers.
Retrieved from:
https://www.caymancompass.com/2011/08/10/woman-fined-for-selling-numbers/

'Elections Office prepares for single-member constituencies.' (26 October 2015)
Retrieved from: http://www.caymaniantimes.ky/elections-office-prepares-for-single-member-constituencies

CPSIA information can be obtained
at www.ICGtesting.com
Printed in the USA
LVHW021920190521
687904LV00014B/929